Ants? In My Pants?

for Barbara, Peter and Kitty

Ants? In My Pants?

An Antimated Tayle by Kahanni Bahz

Principal Illustrations by Kevin Fraser

Additional Illustrations by Andrew Gooderham, Paul Neale & Gavin Buchanan

Published by Tawhl Tayles Press Inc.

Canadian Cataloguing in Publication Data

Bahz, Kahanni
    Ants? In my pants?

ISBN 0-9683654-0-X

I. Fraser, Kevin. II. Title.

PS8553.A344A77 1998   jC811'.54   C98-931015-9
PR9199.3.B324A77 1998

First Edition
10 9 8 7 6 5 4 3 2 1

Tawhl Tayles Press Inc.
34 Armstrong Avenue
Georgetown, Ontario
Canada L7G 4R9

Website: www.antsinmypants.com

Acknowledgements
This is the first imprint of a new book by a new publisher. It represents years of determination, disappointment, and sometimes despair in pursuing a dream. More than anything, however, it represents just what can be accomplished when people encourage and help one another. The following people are among the many without whom this book would not be possible.

Alex Heinz, Paul Allems & Kim Hartford, Lynn Campbell, Lynda Pogue, Lois Fraser, Laurie Gelfand, Ric Amis, Diane Taylor, Biri Sodhi, Xandra Kendall, Doug Pattison, Theresa Ritter, Gavin Buchanan, Benjamin Koo, Theresa Tunnell, Paul Neale, Stephen McPherson, Jayne MacKinlay, Kevin Fraser, Andrew Gooderham, Nick Kammer & Ellen Powers, Chuck Havill, Frederick Innis, and Third Stone Productions.

Thank you all,
Neil Holland, Alpha Ant, Tawhl Tayles Press Inc.

Credits
Book Design: J. Lynn Campbell
Art Direction: Neil Holland
Editors: Carroll Gair, Alex Heinz

Color separation by Rainbow Digicolor Inc., Toronto
Printed and bound in Hong Kong, China by
Book Art Inc., Toronto

Introduction

As I write this introduction, more than five years have passed since I first conceived of the story. My first thoughts then, were of a fidgeting boy confronted by an impatient photographer. From this kernel, memories of my own childhood began to interweave with experiences as a parent to my own uniquely wonderful son.

As an artist, I hoped to create a book that would challenge and stimulate older children who were capable of reading 'chapter books,' but still enjoyed having pictures as part of the story. But as a parent, I envisioned wide-eyed children, of all ages, warmly nestled at bedtime, intently listening to a loved one's voice.

As to whether I have brought these romantic notions to fruition, I can't say. I do, however, know that, in reviewing my handiwork, I have a deeper understanding of how special each child is and how uniquely different each interprets the world.

Let us delight in our children, for all the wonder of them.

Kahanni Bahz
March 1998

"What *are* you wearing?
Your clothes are all rumpled."
My mother said, "People will stare,
at a boy who looks crumpled.

Go back to your room.
Those clothes will not do!
Today for your pictures,
you'll wear something new.

A new shirt and jacket,
laid out on your chair,
with *special* pants,
in which you'll look fair."

I went back to my room,
and put on the new clothes,
then looked in the mirror,
to strike my mean pose.

What I expected,
oh, heaven knows,
you just can't imagine,
how I *hated* those clothes!

"You'll be the envy of all,"
Mother said, as she entered my room.
But the thought of being seen,
filled me with doom.

"My friends like me fine,
but Mother," said I, Billy,
"if I'm seen in these pants,
they'll just think I'm silly."

Each year at this time,
new clothes are the scene,
but for pictures this year,
in *these* clothes, I wouldn't be seen.

A disguise was called for,
I'd wear a long coat and hat.
It would be a detective,
that people looked at.

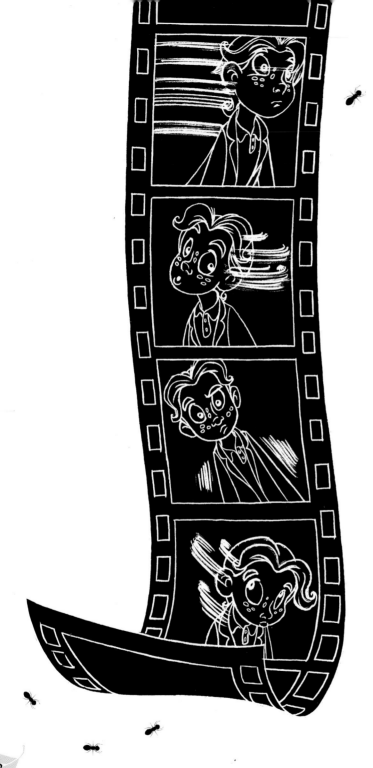

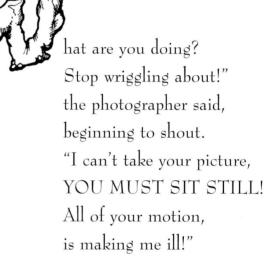

hat are you doing?
Stop wriggling about!"
the photographer said,
beginning to shout.
"I can't take your picture,
YOU MUST SIT STILL!
All of your motion,
is making me ill!"

"This chair is *too* hard,"
I said in mid squirm.
"It's not to my liking,
Must it be so firm?"

The photographer cried,
"The problem is ants!
This boy is a boy,
with ants in his pants!"

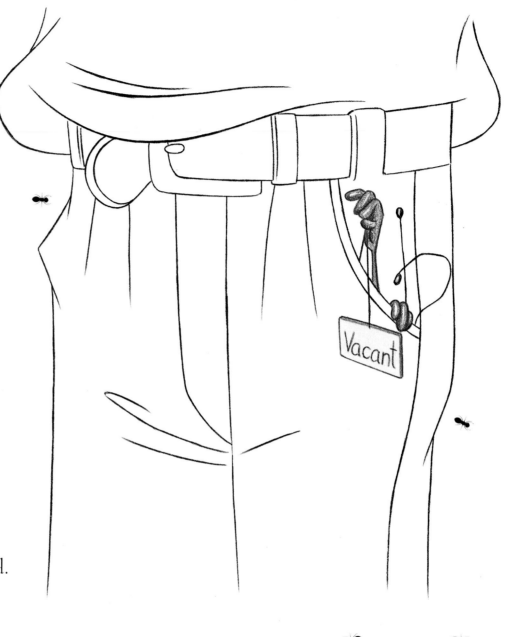

My eyes opened wide,
at the mention of ants.
They have their place,
but not in my pants!

When Mother had told me,
these were *special* pants,
I hadn't expected,
their *feature* was *ants*.

"Are there any ants in there?" I asked.
No answer my hope.
But my question was answered,
with a chorus of, "Nope!"

ack to the class,
with a stiff-legged gait,
my brain busy thinking,
what a cruel twist of fate.

When I asked for some pets,
in mind were some mice.
For some cute furry rodents,
I'd have thanked Mother twice.

"Hey you ants!
This *arrangement* won't do.
I can't wear these pants,
while sharing them too.
I know you're in there.
You'd better come out.
Don't try to ignore me.
Don't make me shout!"

Out of my pocket,
popped a tiny round head,
that shushed me, and whispered,
"We're all in bed!"

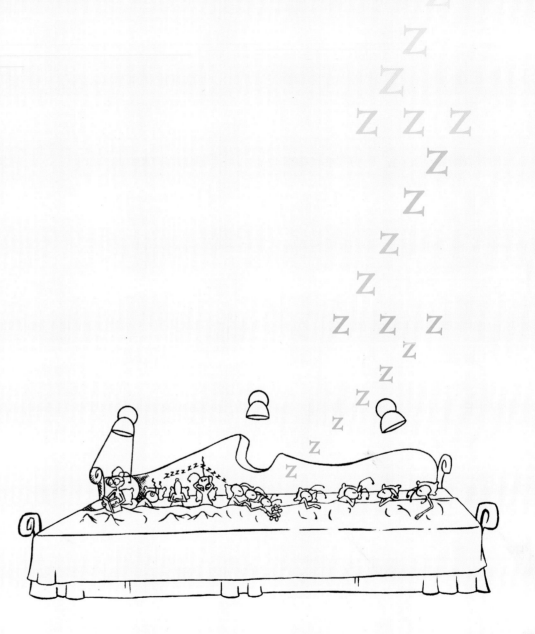

I could tell by its smirk,
the ant was telling a lie.
No way could it fool me,
but it was *determined* to try.

"Who *are* you?" I asked,
my pretense, to cope.
The ant answered lightly,
"An *ant*, who is Gope."

This ant was a tease,
with a name, such as Gope,
to think I'd believe it,
it must *too*, be a dope.

The ant was not happy.
I had done it wrong.
For making fun of its name,
it scolded me strong.

"Gope is an old name,
though different it's true,
not one to make fun of,
though familiar or new."

"I'm sorry," I said,
"I didn't mean to offend,
but, solve my problem,
I'll call you friend."

"*What* is your problem?
Oh, *do* tell me do!
Gope loves solutions,
but problems are few."

"*You* are my problem,
and the other ants, too.
Leaving would solve it,
so good riddance to you!"

FOR SALE
SOLD

Fraser & Holland · Realtor

"Oh joy, what excitement!"
Gope squealed out in glee.
"There are *two* problems,
if you expect *us* to flee.

These pants are our home,
they *suit us* quite well,
but if you find us a new one,
we might be *willing* to sell."

This ant was a trickster,
and not welcome to stay.
And to think for *these* trousers,
I'd be willing to pay!

I'll teach Gope a lesson.
Oh boy, how I'll try,
to find a great home,
one *they'll* be willing to buy.

"I have it! It's perfect!
Just you wait, Gope, and see.
Our class has an ant farm,
that's this moment free.
It's got a reeeal tiny barn,
and dirt to tunnel through,
with walls of glass,
each room has a view."

My hopes of a quick sale,
to be, were not to be.
Gope took one look,
then shook his head at me.

"Nope, it's not home,
I do not like it at all."
Gope said, "For an ant,
it's much too small."

'Invertebrate Gothic' Ant Wood

"What *are* you eating?
It smells divine."
Gope called out dryly,
"We're ready to dine.
Don't bother to serve us,
a few crumbs will do.
I'll gather the morsels,
oh, drop them, please do."

My troubles were many.
I needed some rest.
What I got was demands,
to serve lunch, to a pest.

"No, Gope," said I,
"it's not going to happen.
I'm too troubled to feed you.
On me, you won't fatten."

The ant's eyes twinkled,
no hint of dismay.
Of my refusal to serve,
Gope had this to say.
"To be troubled by troubles,
is not very funny.
What you need is to laugh,
then you'll feel sunny."

Gope winked and was gone,
as I started to eat,
awaiting more trouble,
when something tickled my feet.
I tried hard not to laugh,
but I started to jiggle,
then snorts like a pig,
grew into a giggle.

The whole class now watching,
mouths open, wide eyed,
I continued to eat,
casting food, all about, as I tried.

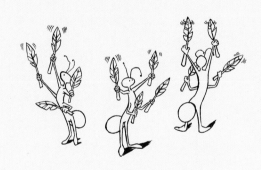

27

Hysterical laughter followed by hiccuping along with the usual crazy behavior.
Ms M.

note, I was given,
by my teacher, Ms Mazy,
to visit the nurse,
for fear I'd gone crazy.
I tried to explain,
as I started to hiccup,
the ants were to blame,
wanting lunch, they could pick up.

Ms Mazy put my arms in the air,
as she sent me from class,
saying I should hold my breath,
until the hiccups pass.

My troubles many, grew again,
when seen by Principal Whickup,
for in my eyes, she thought, she saw,
the victim of a stick-up.
She flattened out against the wall,
and asked, "How many are they?"
I told her, "Very funny, ma'am,
but I haven't time to play."

The nurse ducked behind her desk,
when sight of me she caught,
asking, "How many are they?"
I replied, "You're very funny...not!"

The nurse read my note and said,
"Hmmm...so you've been afflicted, Giggle-itus,
followed closely by the dreaded,
Hiccups-un-invite-us.

Ms Mazy picked a classic cure,
your hiccups, well in hand,
but the riddle of these giggles,
we have yet to understand."

"Yes, my hiccups are no more,
but the reason, I'll make clear.
It's not by that, which makes *you* play,
but from a fright, I fear."

"I saw myself a grown up,
although a kid today,
I couldn't help but wonder,
if I'd too, be weird someday."

31

ope and I struggled,
matching wits through the day,
before joining the cast,
of our yearly school play.

"This is exciting!"
Gope said, "What a thrill!
To be part of a play,
I can hardly sit still."

"Oh, I hate this day," said I,
"there's been no fun for me.
Now, my talents for acting,
wasted dressed as a tree.
A swash-buckled pirate,
or brave knight, to a dragon, sent to slay,
these are the roles,
I'm most suited to play."

So I asked the director,
for a more worthy part.
To plead my case,
I said this, from the heart.
"I can't believe it!
Is this all a big joke?
Can I really expect,
a career as an oak?"

"There are no small parts,"
the director replied,
"only small actors!"
quoting a saying, with wisdom implied.

"I get it," said Gope.
"It's meaning is clear.
The amount of your effort,
will make the audience cheer."

"A tree made exciting,
yah right Gope, as if!
Far from good drama,
they're really, quite stiff.
What kind of an effort,
could bring life to a tree?
I'm miserable Gope,
my stardom, not, to be."

"Now don't you despair"
ordered the ant.
"What you need is direction,
to bring life to your plant.
A tree is not stiff,
as the wind makes it dance.
Gope the director,
will be the wind in your pants."

Gope did not answer,
when for some peace, I did beg.
Then all of a sudden,
I felt a pinch, on my leg.
I tried to be still.
I really did fight.
I twitched and I jerked,
but they started to bite.

Side to side I began to thrash,
my branches all about,
actors running to and fro,
the director began to shout.

"What are you doing?
You're ruining my play!
Never in the history of theatre,
has a tree behaved in this way."

My branches now bare,
I blurted out my confession.
"The ants were to blame,
for this artistic impression."

Later, at supper,
Mother asked, "Why aren't you eating?"
As Father went on,
about his afternoon meeting.

I continued to push food,
'round my plate,
as Mother described a client,
she really did hate.
Mom and Dad had no problems,
when compared to my day,
so they raised their glasses,
and made a toast, "Thank God, it's Friday."

"How was your day, Billy?"
Mother finally did ask.
"Okay, I guess," was my reply,
the trouble to tell, too great a task.

The discussion then shifted,
to plans for the weekend,
of gardening, tennis, and golf,
on the weather would depend.

The subject his garden,
Father was talking and talking,
of the battle he'd won,
over ants he'd been stalking.
How proudly he went on,
yakity yak, yakity yak,
and I thought of a train,
'clickity clack, clickity clack.'

Until Mother spoke up,
it was she, not he,
that had found the solution,
to a garden ant free!

Then to me she winked,
my mood, suddenly solemn,
to think my pants,
an end to Dad's ant problem.

I couldn't believe it,
this a mother would do?
But her wink was the proof,
it *must* be true.

So I sat and I thought,
and I thought as I steamed.
The ants were *their* problem,
so I planned and I schemed.

L ater that night,
alone in my room,
thinking of problems,
in a sorcerer's gloom.

I thought of the wrongs,
that were needing a right,
starting when Dad,
was robbed of his fight.
The ants were his bane.
His challenge to meet.
But Mom's interference,
amounts to defeat.

Dad's time in the garden,
was a trouble to Mom,
but her manner of coping,
was just plain wrong.

So now I've Gope,
my pants as his nest.
And outsmarting this trickster,
has been quite a test.

These slacks I so hate,
in the closet would stay,
but for Mother's insistence,
I wear them each school day.
It took me some time,
and a great deal of thought,
before a device I cooked up,
in a deliciously devious plot.

 said good-bye to the day,
later that night,
feeling warm and secure,
in my bed tucked tight.
The ants' eyes upon me,
watching me sleep,
in pairs by the hundred,
through darkness did peep.

I began dreaming of clothes,
that were out to get me,
in league with the ants,
to try and upset me.

Shirts flew about,
as though they had wings,
buzzing my head,
bumping my things.
Socks that were jumping,
bounced on my bed,
while pants stood lurking,
as something to dread.

44

Then on went a light,
and everything stopped,
lit up was a stage,
on which Gope had just popped.
Along with a big band,
that jazzed into noise,
when Gope called out,
"1, 2, 3... HIT IT BOYZ!"

Such a sight, I'd never seen!
To the rhythm of the racket,
my clothes began to dance.
Led by Gope, in his sparkling jacket.

I stood up on my bed,
against the music to yell,
but was tripped by the socks,
that howled as I fell.
I sailed through the air,
in a headlong dive,
with a crash and a bang,
to the floor did arrive.

The party was over,
now awake from my dream,
but still through the dark,
the ants' eyes did gleam.

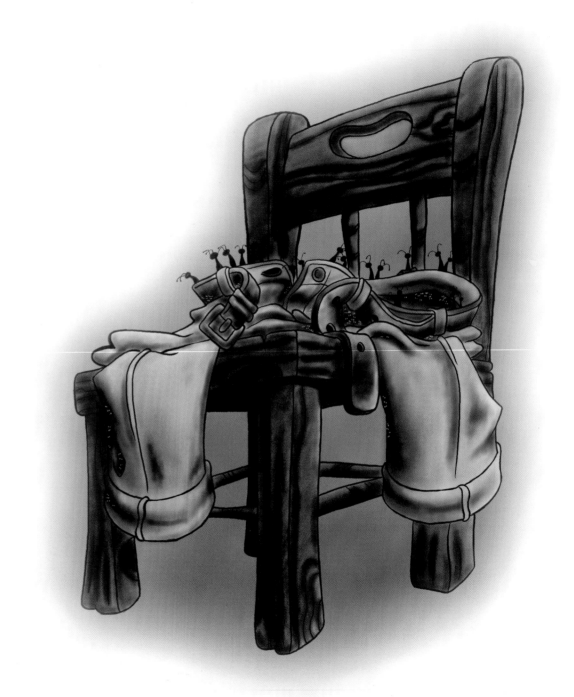

Then my door swung open,
and my parents appeared,
whose eyes fell upon me,
with looks that seared.
Of noise and commotion,
for answers did press,
to them my room a disaster,
and not just a mess.

Each fired questions,
in tones that were stern,
with looks round the room,
a meaning to learn.
But I couldn't help them,
I too was dumbfounded.
By the clothes in my dream,
I was totally surrounded.

49

I couldn't explain it.
Was there even a chance?
That it wasn't a dream,
that laundry *could* dance.
Father began laughing,
and was pushed into the hall,
by Mother who scolded,
"You're no help at all."

Big trouble was promised
as Mother did leave,
but if the room was reordered,
I could gain a reprieve.
I wouldn't have long,
until her return,
but on Gope and his allies,
I had tables to turn.
The clock was ticking,
and with a room to settle,
to win a battle with Gope,
now a test of my mettle.

I raced round the room,
and grabbed all the clothes,
then into *those* pants,
stuffed my limp foes.
I packed them in tight,
so they couldn't get free,
then stood the pants up,
like a great big "V".

Then like a blur,
my speed faster than light,
the things on my shelves,
I again set right.
With a bound into bed,
I pulled the sheets to my chin,
not a moment to spare,
as Mother walked in.

51

"Well now," she said,
"your room seems to be clean.
Everything back in its place,
so I've no need to be mean."

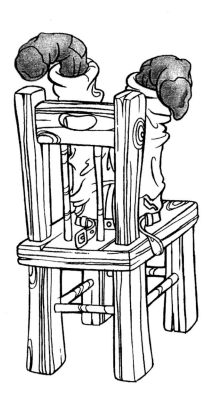

As if struck by lightning,
Mother began to stare,
at the pants in the corner,
upside down on the chair.
"Why are your pants,
arranged in this way?
I don't understand why,
you get stranger each day."

More questions she asked,
while awaiting my answer,
but I eluded her probing,
with the grace of a dancer.
"What pants?" I replied.
"Could you be more specific?"
Mother's eyes just rolled,
my evasion terrific.

She picked up the pants,
and reached inside,
on discovering the laundry,
laughed till she cried.

"Oh Mother," I said,
in my sweetest voice,
"my clothes for tomorrow,
could it be my choice?"

Mother still laughing,
nodded and kissed me good night,
so my plan I began,
when off went the light.

"Sleep tight in your beds,"
I called to the ants,
"with tomorrow awaits you,
a move away from those pants."

55

From the pants there came,
a great hue and cry,
with ants demanding of Gope,
who, what, where, and why!

Then to me, Gope cried, "What a fuss!
Upside down, quite unable to move,
pinned against these pants we are,
until all these clothes you remove."

"Don't you worry Gope," said I,
"I've got just the thing,
a solution to your problem,
whose praises you'll sing.
Those clothes will be loosened,
when in the washer they'll slosh,
as Father says often,
'it all comes out in the wash'."

From the ants there came,
a horrific gasp.
Their fate in the washer,
quickly did grasp.

56

Then a conference they had,
in a collective mutter,
before Gope addressed me,
in a voice smooth as butter.

"And what is this *new* home,
of which you did speak?
We've no interest in leaving,
but our *curiosity* did pique."

Though Gope's tone was cool,
in my device he was snared,
a brave face he put on,
but in my pants was now scared.

With Gope's fate I would play,
as with a mouse and a cat,
I'd sell him his home,
but at a price that is fat.
"It's a *beautiful* garden
where you'd be happy,
so much *more* than a home,
an address that's snappy."

"But..." I said, "I'm not so sure,
if you're the right sort of ant.
Everyone wants the best address,
but of course...can't."

"The right sort of ant?"
Gope said with a snort.
"Why...we're the best kind,
used to the finest in comfort."

I let Gope go on,
pleading their case,
for a home in the garden,
did desperately chase.

Finally I said, "You've convinced me,
you'll suit the garden quite nice,
ants of *your* stature,
have no concern for the price.
What would you trade,
for the right to this garden?
A bountiful haven,
at any price, a bargain."

"The pants!" exclaimed Gope,
"No longer with us to share.
You'll get them free and clear.
As a trade, that's fair."

Imagine, Gope the great trickster,
so eager to please.
I just loved it,
the more I could tease.

"How is it fair," I replied,
"when I don't *want* the pants?
They're not to my liking,
with or *without* you ants!"

"What's not to like?"
Gope said, "They're *quite* fine.
The very best of material,
with a crease and a shine."

Then a thought,
like a meteor did hit.
'The shine's what I hate,
not the cut or the fit.'

I knew there was something.
Something I should have seen.
What made those pants silly,
was their high gloss sheen.
This sudden found insight,
put my brain in a twirl.
With revenge set aside,
a new *twist*, did unfurl.

"Gope, it's the shine I dislike,
to remove it, the fee.
For this trade to happen,
a change there must be.
Though it be ant free,
the garden's not free, to ants,
so while the pants glisten,
of a trade, you've no chance."

"Oh yes," said Gope. "Yes!
We're able to trade.
This shine we'll subdue.
Consider them re-made!

I said from the start,
problems were few,
each solution we found,
as the problem we knew.
Now that you've chosen,
this problem to mull,
we'll set about to ensure,
your pants are quite dull."

In the morning I got up,
before Mom or Dad,
with the pants to the garden,
to show the ants their new pad.

Gope liked it just fine,
and his cohorts concurred.
But the trade on a catch, did snag,
that to me had never occurred.

The solution they offered,
was founded in trust.
Gope was a trickster.
Was the deal just a bust?

63

He said what was needed,
was plain old dirt,
a secret stitch and time,
to create slacks that were pert.

But this was not all,
I was expected to swallow,
for the pants I was to put on,
and in the dirt wallow.

"Wait just a minute,"
said I with hands on hips,
"this trade must be concluded,
without tricks or slips.
Mother would kill me,
if in these pants, in mud I did roll.
Your plan is transparent,
your trickery droll.
The dirt will come out,
when Mother washes the pants.
To think your plan would fool me,
you must be the *silliest* sort of ants."

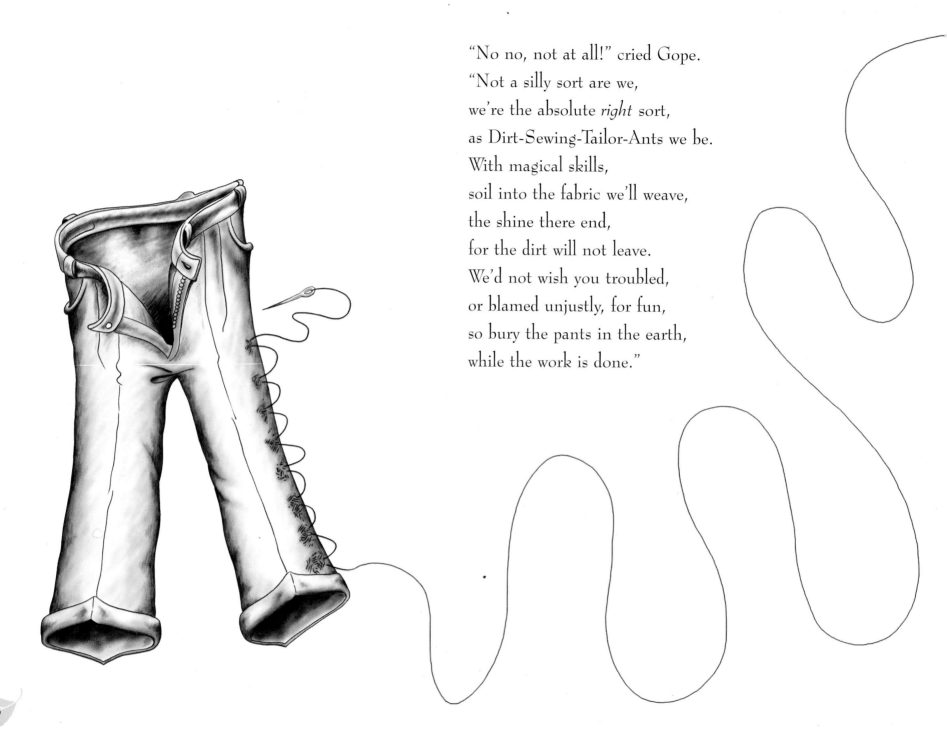

"No no, not at all!" cried Gope.
"Not a silly sort are we,
we're the absolute *right* sort,
as Dirt-Sewing-Tailor-Ants we be.
With magical skills,
soil into the fabric we'll weave,
the shine there end,
for the dirt will not leave.
We'd not wish you troubled,
or blamed unjustly, for fun,
so bury the pants in the earth,
while the work is done."

Gope sounded sincere,
so the pants I planted,
with a farewell to the ants,
peace I was finally granted.

It would take some time,
so I went to relax,
watching Saturday cartoons,
while the ants altered my slacks.

How peaceful it was,
my life trouble free,
one with the world,
all worries behind me.

Mother and Father,
finally got up,
in the kitchen with coffee,
cup after cup.

Mother too, passed through,
on her way to the garden,
though interrupting my show,
she tickled me in the bargain.

Father passed through,
on his way to the garden,
interrupting my show,
he begged for my pardon.
He wasn't out long,
when for my Mother did call,
insisting she just had to see,
the surprise crop of the fall.

I tuned back in to my show,
for my mind to corrupt,
but Mom came back,
like a volcano to erupt.

Then she exploded,
"WHAT HAVE YOU DONE TO YOUR PANTS?"
As Father called out,
"Oh no, there's ants in my plants!"

...the end?